# LOOK OUT, PATRICK!

A Red Fox Book

Published by Random House Children's Books
20 Vauxhall Bridge Road, London SW1V 2SA

A division of Random House UK Ltd
London Melbourne Sydney Auckland
Johannesburg and agencies throughout the world

First published by Hutchinson Children's Books 1990

This edition Red Fox 1992

3 5 7 9 10 8 6 4

Copyright © Paul Geraghty 1990

Printed and bound in Singapore by
Tien Wah Press (Pte) Ltd

RANDOM HOUSE UK Limited Reg. No. 954009

ISBN 0 09 910981 6

# LOOK OUT, PATRICK!

## Paul Geraghty

RED FOX

For Althea

Thanks to the Moppets for naming Patrick

One breezy afternoon Patrick
was strolling home.

It was a lovely day, the birds were singing
and there was a spring in his step.
'The world is such a pleasant place,' he said.

**OH NO, PATRICK! LOOK OUT!**

He gazed about in wonder.
The countryside was full of
delightful suprises:

the smell of new grass, the fresh green leaves and ripe red berries just ready to eat.

**OH NO, PATRICK! LOOK OUT!**

He bent down to sniff at a buttercup.

Bumble bees were buzzing back and forth busily. The air was sweet with the scent of nectar.

**OH NO, PATRICK! LOOK OUT!**

A butterfly tickled his whiskers, and in the background water gurgled. Patrick's tummy began gurgling too.

I wonder what's cooking in the cottage, he thought.

**OH NO, PATRICK! LOOK OUT!**

He tiptoed carefully. That wicked cat might be on the prowl.

There was no sign of the cat. But there *was* a nice big chunk of cheese.

'Mmmmm,' said Patrick.
'Just the thing.'

**OH NO, PATRICK! LOOK OUT!**

Just then a delicious smell drifted by.
'Even better!' said Patrick.

'I wonder what it is.'

**OH NO, PATRICK! LOOK OUT!**

He followed his nose as it twitched and whiffed and pointed and sniffed. But suddenly...

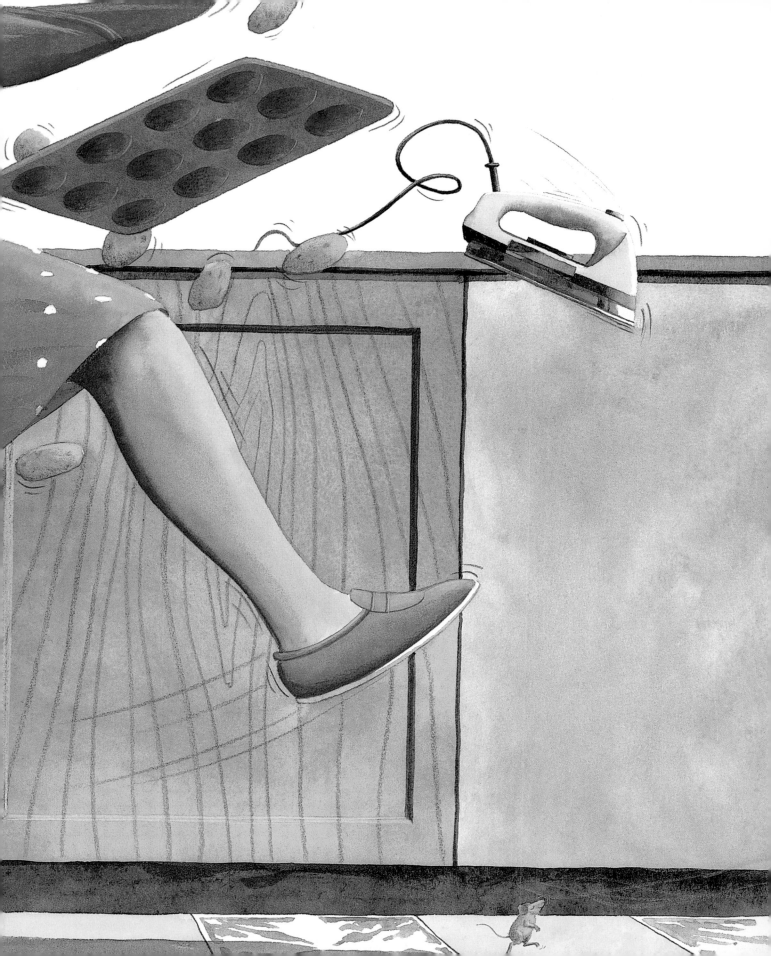

OH NO, PATRICK! LOOK OUT!

'Phew!
Must be my lucky day!'

# Some bestselling Red Fox picture books